How this book works

The story of **A Bus for Miss Moss** has been written for you to read with your child. You take turns to read:

You read these words.

Miss Moss, Miss Moss could never keep still.

Miss Moss had a mill on a hill.

Your child reads these words.

You don't have to finish the story in one session. If your child is getting tired, use the ribbon marker to pause and come back to it later.

You can find out more about helping your child with this book, and with reading in general, on pages 30-31.

A Bus
for
Miss Moss

Turn the page to start the story.

Miss Moss, Miss Moss
could never keep still.

Miss Moss had
a mill on a hill.

She worked so hard,
milling sack after sack...

6

Bad luck!
Miss Moss had
a bad back.

"I think it is time to sell my mill."

"I cannot mill
if I am ill."

So she moved house —
and what a shock!

Miss Moss had
a hut on a rock.

She lay in bed with
a terrible cough –

"I had a sun deck but it fell off."

"And there's no sun when the fog comes up."

"I am sick of fog –
I am fed up!"

Now she lives in the meadow
right next to us:

MISS
MOSS 3

Miss Moss has a bed in a bus.

With trees in an orchard,
one to ten...

A pig in a pen,
and a duck
and a hen.

And it's easy to go
on a trip, you know –

"I can pack up
and off I go."

Miss Moss is better,
she sits in the sun.

Miss Moss has
a lot of fun.

Puzzle 1

Read the sentences and say whether you think Miss Moss is happy or sad.

1.

Miss Moss had a mill on a hill.

2.

"I cannot mill if I am ill."

3.

Miss Moss had
a hut on a rock.

4.

Miss Moss has
a lot of fun.

You could have fun talking about what it would be like to live in a bus.

Puzzle 2

There is one wrong word in the sentences below each picture. What should they say?

1.

Bad duck! Miss Moss had a bad back.

2.

"I had a run deck but it fell off."

3.

"I am sick of fig –
I am fed up!"

4.

"I cat pack up
and off I go."

Puzzle 3

Look at the picture, then read the words below. Which five things are in the picture?

- a bus
- a cat
- a dog
- a doll
- a duck

- a hat
- a hen
- a net
- a pig
- a sack

Answers to puzzles

Puzzle 1

1.

2.

3.

4.

Puzzle 2

1. Bad ~~duck~~!
   Bad luck!

2. I had a ~~fun~~ deck.
   I had a sun deck.

3. I am sick of ~~fig~~.
   I am sick of fog.

4. I ~~eat~~ pack up.
   I can pack up.

Puzzle 3

a bus   a hat   a duck

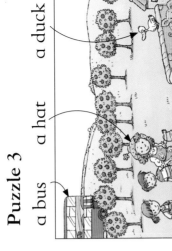

a hen   a pig

Guidance notes

Usborne Very First Reading is a series of fifteen books, specially developed for children who are learning to read. In the first seven books, you and your child take turns to read, and your child steadily builds the knowledge and confidence to read alone.

The words for your child to read in **A Bus for Miss Moss** introduce these seven letters or letter-combinations:

Your child will soon grasp that **ff** has the same sound as **f**, **ll** as **l** and **ss** as **s**. These are often among the first letters that children learn to read at school. Later books in the series gradually introduce more letters, sounds and spelling patterns, while reinforcing the ones your child already knows.

You'll find lots more information about the structure of the series, advice on helping your child with reading, extra practice activities and games on the Very First Reading website,* **www.usborne.com/veryfirstreading**

*US readers go to **www.veryfirstreading.com**

Some questions and answers

- **Why do I need to read with my child?**
  Sharing stories and taking turns makes reading an enjoyable and fun activity for children. It also helps them to develop confidence and reading stamina, and to take part in an exciting story using very few words.

- **When is a good time to read?**
  Choose a time when you are both relaxed, but not too tired, and there are no distractions. Only read for as long as your child wants to – you can always try again another day.

- **What if my child gets stuck?**
  Don't simply read the problem word yourself, but prompt your child and try to find the right answer together. Similarly, if your child makes a mistake, go back and look at the word together. Don't forget to give plenty of praise and encouragement.

- **We've finished, now what do we do?**
  It's a good idea to read the story several times to give your child more practice and more confidence. Then, when your child is ready, you can go on to the next book in the series, **Dog Diary.**

Edited by Jenny Tyler and Lesley Sims
Designed by Russell Punter

First published in 2010 by Usborne Publishing Ltd., Usborne House,
83-85 Saffron Hill, London EC1N 8RT, England. www.usborne.com
Copyright © 2010 Usborne Publishing Ltd.

USBORNE VERY FIRST READING

There are fifteen titles in the **Usborne Very First Reading** series, which has been specially developed to help children learn to read.

To find out more about the structure of the series, go to **www.usborne.com/veryfirstreading**

1   2   3

4   5   6